A LOVE WAR:

TWISTED

R. D. Solomon Jr.

A LOVE WAR: TWISTED

Printed in the United States of America

ISBN-13:978-0692701058
ISBN-10:0692701052

Printed by Createspace 2016
Published by BlaqRayn Publishing Plus 2016

Dedication

To the most loving, caring and hardworking

woman I knew, Hattie Williams Moore

&

Tyrone Marquette Smith, a selfless, loving

man, the epitome what real men aspire to be;

the man I loved and admired as my own

father.

I love and miss you both dearly.

TABLE OF CONTENTS

A Love War: TWISTED

Chapter 1: Fed Up

"I had a good time bae; we need to do that again." It was a cool spring night in Savannah, GA as Justin walked Nicole back home while talking about the state of their relationship. Justin had a good time also and wanted to spend more time with Nicole, but he knew that being able to spend a lot of quality time with her would be extremely difficult considering they were both married. Something Nicole doesn't know about him.

"I work all next week, so I'll let you know when, but there is something I do want to talk to you about."

A Love War: TWISTED

Sensing the agitation in his voice, Nicole knew where the conversation was headed.

"Okay, just call me bae. I need to get in the house. Tyrell will be home soon. I don't want to get busted." She hastily said, trying to rush into the house.

Justin was tired of living this way, trying his best to get her to understand.

"That's what I'm talking about. I'm about to erupt man! That's my boy but aren't you happier with me? The way I take you out, pamper you, even rub your feet? And you know you love the "D".You should leave him and be with me!"

A Love War: TWISTED

Still trying to get into the house, Nicole tried rushing the conversation along,

"Bae stop please...this isn't the time for this. I'll call you around 10:15. He'll be asleep by then and we can talk. When he asks me where I'm going I'll just say I'm going for a walk."

She felt her phone vibrate.

"Shit, he just called. Bae, I gotta go." She tried to walk away hurriedly but he pulled her back.

"Okay. Fine, but let me taste those lips before you go. And I just want you to know...until I have you I won't stop."

She tried convincing him that this was the wrong time to talk to Tyrell, but one-day things will be the way they fantasized it to be.

"In due time baby. I have to let him down easy so it doesn't seem all for naught. Bye."

"Bye."

He said as he walked away feeling totally defeated .

A Love War: TWISTED

Chapter 2: Heated

Trying to figure out the best way to break the news to Tyrell, Nicole asked God for direction.

"Lord, guide me. Let me make the right decision with no regrets or indiscretion. I love Tyrell but I'm in love with Justin. I think I'll wait a while before I tell him, but there's no way to avoid the fussing... pain... Torment...the sense of betrayal. They had to be best friends...I hope this has a peaceful end..."

Tyrell heard her as he walked in the house from work.

"Hey bae, who are you talking to? Don't tell me you've gone crazy..."

A Love War: TWISTED

Startled by his voice, she looked around and said.

"No baby, I was talking to God. But I am crazy...about you."

With a big smile, he pulled Nicole close in a tight embrace.

"I love you too baby. You are so amazing. Did you try a new perfume? It doesn't smell like it's for a lady...."

She'd forgotten how extremely close she and Justin had been while they were together. She realized she should have taken a quick shower before Tyrell got home. She had to think of a quick lie.

"No sweetie, my boss got happy and hugged me. I've been smelling it all day.

The smell really bugs me. I'm going to take a shower now. We will talk after I'm done."

Detecting her withdrawn attitude towards him and knowing his own need and desire to be with his wife, he pleaded for her time and attention.

"But all I need is few minutes, maybe even one. Lately you've been so distant. It hasn't been mentioned because I wanted to see if it was a phase, but it isn't...is it? Something is definitely wrong... What's really going on?"

Trying to sound concerned and not too dismissive towards his feelings she said,

"Nothing is going on. What are you talking about bae? Come on...we have two beautiful kids and a life people dream of. A bank account people wish for and can't even speak of. What do you think has changed? Come on..talk to me." They walked over to the sofa and sat down as he began to express how he felt.

"Well, we argue all of the time, we don't talk anymore and obviously you're seeing someone else. These aren't things I've recently felt..."

As he talked, he noticed a piece of jewelry that he hadn't bought her and a hickey he didn't place on her. At the sight of those things, he jumped up from the sofa in an outrage.

A Love War: TWISTED

"Who bought you the necklace around your neck and look at that hickey, or is that a welt!?!"

Becoming infuriated at the accusations and still not ready to reveal the truth, she started an argument to save face.

"Fuck you! I don't have to listen to these allegations! I don't know what your problem is or what your infatuation is with my body but I'm sorry it's not perfect or to your liking! I have flaws you know! If you don't like it bite me!"

"Nobody said anything about your body. Chill. What the fuck is wrong with you? I just asked a question. I'm sorry.. no more arguing. Let's calla truce. Come on. Let's take a shower together."

No longer wanting to talk or be around him, Nicole said, "I'm going for a walk. It may make me feel better."

"Well I'm going with you."

"Stay the fuck away from me!" Nicole yelled.

What did you say to me!?! Tyrell yelled back.

"You heard me, Satan's seed..."

"Okay then...cool. Bye. You're straight with me." Tyrell said as Nicole walked out of the door, slamming it behind her.

A Love War: TWISTED

Chapter 3: Trouble

Still flustered by the argument, Nicole called Justin to calm her nerves as she walked back home. She needed someone she could confide in since she obviously couldn't talk to Tyrell.

"Hello?"

Despite being half sleep, Justin managed to answer Nicole's call on the first ring.

"Baby, please talk to me. Me and that bastard just got through arguing!"

Due to the urgency in her voice, Justin shook off his sleep, sat up in bed and tried his best to help solve her problem.

A Love War: TWISTED

"Okay, calm down, you know I'm here for you. Talk to me baby. What can I do?"

"Just talk to me. This is something that I have to deal with." Nicole didn't need a "Mr. Fix-It" right now; she just needed someone to listen to her.

"Do I need to come by and tell him some real shit?" Justin asked still wanting to help her solve the issue.

"No bae, but I'm almost back to the house. When is the next time we can go out?" She said, assuring him she just needed to vent and some time with him. She would be glad herself when she mustered up the courage to tell Tyrell the truth about her relationship with Justin.This whole thing was overwhelming her.

"I told you I'll let you know.. damn! Why are you sweating me!?!"

Still hiding his own marital status, Justin felt if Nicole would just leave Tyrell already they could be together. He wouldn't have to continue sneaking behind his best friend's back to be with her.

"I just asked a fuckin question! Fuck it. I'll let it be... bye."

As she was walking into the driveway, she saw Tyrell talking to someone in a car she didn't recognize. She made a mental note to bring it up the second they stepped back in the house.

A Love War: TWISTED

"Alright, I'll see you later. Talk to you soon." Tyrell said to the driver of the car.

Nicole was pissed off now and yelled frantically as soon as they entered the house, "Who the fuck was that!?! I can't fucking believe you!"

The kids were asleep and Tyrell didn't want to wake them; plus he and Nicole had been arguing since he got home from work and he was tired of it so he said,

"None of your damn business, just like you always tell me. I'm not about to argue anymore though. T.J. and Monica are asleep" as he walked away into their bedroom.

A Love War: TWISTED

Walking behind him and seeing that she wasn't going to get any answers about the person he was talking to, she just changed the subject.

"Well speaking of Monica, she asked me to go out, so I am going with her. I need to get out of this house."

Going out and having fun with her best friend was all she needed to take her mind off of all of her problems in and out of home.

"Whatever, have fun. Justin is coming over anyway. Hurry up and leave so we can chill and watch the game."

A Love War: TWISTED

As Nicole was leaving the room, Tyrell's son T.J., who was now awake, entered.

"Hey T.J.! How's my little man? Can't sleep? Let me tuck you in and I'll teach you to count sheep." Nicole said as T.J. walked to her.

"You love being a stepmom, but you hate being a wife...how nice....Whelp, I asked for this life." Tyrell mumbled under his breath.

"What did you say!?!" She yelled as she laid her phone on the bed.

"Nothing." He replied as he lays his phone on the bed.

A Love War: TWISTED

"I'll be back in a minute bae." She responded as she went to lie T.J. back down and help him fall back asleep.

"Okay. I'm headed downstairs to watch a movie until Justin gets here. Do what you want. I don't care."

"Okay, I'm changing clothes then I'm leaving. T.J. is asleep"

"Have a nice evening." He said to Nicole.

While heading downstairs, he noticed that now Monica, his daughter, is awake.

"Monica, are you and T.J. taking turns getting up? Did y'all have candy or something? What's up?"

A Love War: TWISTED

"Daddy I went to your room and you weren't there. I thought that's where you and mommy always are. When I didn't see you I got scared, but your phone was on the bed, so it led me to you." She said as she mistakenly hands him Nicole's phone, which is identical to his.

Laughing at his daughter's response, he asked,

"How baby?".

"I don't know, but I found you." She answered.

"Thank you baby, now off to bed."

"I love you daddy!"

"I love you too bighead."

A Love War: TWISTED

As Monica headed back to bed, Nicole walked in. "I'm gone."

"Okay baby, you got your key?" Tyrell asked.

"Yeah, but I might not be back tonight."

"You know what... just leave. Tell your girl Monica I said hey."

"Bye bae...Damn..."

"Yep. Do you have your phone?"

"Yes, I have my phone! Bye nigga! I'm gone!"

Tired of the back and forth, Tyrell just stated, "Bye man...bye" as Nicole walked out the door.

A Love War: TWISTED

Chapter 4: The Realization

"Finally man! The game we've been waiting for! Who are you going for?"

Justin and Tyrell were supposed to be watching the Los Angeles Lakers and Golden State Warriors game, but Tyrell was lost in his thoughts.

"Huh? My bad man. I'm thinking about Nicole. All she wants to do is argue lately. I know something is wrong and the fussing is getting old."

"She's probably stressed out from work or just tired altogether. It's been 8 years for y'all man. Y'all have been through every type of weather. This is just another storm. It's here to make y'all better. Give her some time. Things will go back to the norm."

"I hope you're right man. I can't continue to do this alone. One more fight and I promise she's gone..."

In mid-sentence, the phone vibrates and Tyrell notices a name appear that he didn't recognize.

"Who the fuck is this!?! Who the fuck is Ramone!?! This can't be my phone...that cheating bitch! Justin, can you watch the kids!?!"

"Calm down man. Why would I need to do that? Where you going?"

"To bring her ass home from Sids'."

"What about the game?"

A Love War: TWISTED

"I've already been played!!! Don't you see?!!! She's probably at the club right now in the bathroom getting laid!"

"Well, bring the kids with us. You know I'm not good with kids. If you're going, we're all going to Sids'."

"Okay, fuck it, cool. Man I don't know what to do..."

"Can't help you on this one bro. On this, I have no clue..."

"Come on."

Fuming, Tyrell grabs the kids from their beds and they all get in the car and head to Sids'.

On the other side of town at the club, Nicole and Monica are on the dance floor dancing to Time of Our Lives by Ne-Yo and Pitbull.

"This club is jumpin' tonight! What do you think Bestie?" Nicole asked Monica.

"Is it too much smoke in here, or is it just me?"

"Okay, yeah it is a little too smoky. Put it this way though, it hides that spot on your dress and you're not choking!"

"That shit ain't funny; the spot was your fault."

"Nobody told you to bump me and spill my drink. That's your fault."

"Whatever. Hey, is that Tyrell at the door!?!"

A Love War: TWISTED

Nicole turned and saw Tyrell standing at the door looking around.

"What the fuck is he doing here!?! Probably finding his whore…"

"What do you mean?" Monica asked, puzzled by Nicole's brusque statement.

"I'll tell you later."

Tyrell soon spotted Nicole and Monica on the danc efloor. He brushed pass everyone, making his way to Nicole to demand answers about this Ramone person calling her phone.

"We need to talk."

"I'm listening." Nicole replied with a nonchalant attitude.

"Outside and give me my phone." Tyrell demanded.

"Excuse me!?!"

"Is that what you said to Ramone!?!" Tyrell yelled as they walked outside where Justin was standing.

Taking deep breaths, Tyrell calmly speaks to everyone.

"I think if there are secrets, we all get them out now."

"Okay, what's going on?" Monica asked, still oblivious to what is going on.

"Monica, don't act innocent now." Tyrell said.

"What do you mean Tyrell? What she got to do with this?"

A Love War: TWISTED

Justin was aware that Tyrell suspected Nicole of cheating, but he didn't understand how Monica got stuck in the middle of this madness unfolding.

By this time, Tyrell is extremely aggravated about how naive everyone is pretending to be.

"Really Mr. Clueless...the same thing you have to do with it! Do I look like I sleep on mine!?! Am I in an eternal slumber!?! Ramone is fake man!!!! I know this is your number! I should fuck you up! But I have to be a father to my children. Hey Monica, how's the house? You know, the one we used to live in!?!"

A Love War: TWISTED

Nicole was now even more furious with Tyrell than she was before. She was relieved that he finally knew the truth about her and Justin because now she could move on with her life, but to know that he'd hidden knowing her best friend in more ways than one was unacceptable.

"What the fuck are you talking about!?! Tyrell, you've gone overboard. You're doing too much! Don't say another word! We are over! But is there another way you and Monica know each other!?!"

Justin couldn't believe how stupid Nicole was acting. Yelling at her he said,

A Love War: TWISTED

"Dumb bitch! It's obvious they at least used to talk! I knew fucking with you came at a cost".

Laughing at his best friend and soon to be ex-wife, knowing they didn't even know what else was in store to be revealed Tyrell said.

"One more surprise. Are you ready for this brother? Tell them Monica!"

She quietly replied. "I'm T.J. and Monica's mother..."

Justin couldn't believe his ears. "What the fuck man! Let's release all the cats from the bag then man! This is going to be scary but..."

A Love War: TWISTED

Knowing what Justin was about to reveal she quickly cut him off.

"Justin don't!" She begged him to be quiet.

Justin couldn't hold it in any longer, since Tyrell was enlightening everyone on the secrets they had been withholding from one another he decided to come clean himself.

"What? You don't want them to know we are married!?! Tyrell, since you fucked my wife I'm going to take your kids!"

"You mean my kids... and I'll see you in court Tyrell!" Monica stated

A Love War: TWISTED

"Go to hell! Nicole, have fun walking home girl" Tyrell said.

"I ain't coming home...I'm getting a hotel after coming from the hospital. I feel sick." She replied.

Grasping the seriousness of the situation, Justin said, "I think we all need to get tested quickly! This is bullshit! Monica let's go home."

"I'm going home. Get your shit. You're gone."

Monica couldn't believe Justin actually thought she would stay with him after what just went down.

"Fuck you then!"

A Love War: TWISTED

Disgusted by the whole situation, Tyrell had one more thing to say before walking to his car and taking his kids home.

"I think we have done enough of that to each other. Justin, you were my brother. Monica, you are my children's mother. All of this definitely leaves us all a little distorted but fuck it. I'm taking my kids home. I'll see you all in court then."

With that being said, they all went their separate ways.

A Love War: TWISTED

Chapter 5: The Aftermath

The next morning, while Tyrell is driving the kids to school, T.J. and Monica begin to ask about Nicole.

"Daddy, where's mommy? I miss her." T.J. says.

"Yea daddy, where's mommy? I miss her. I miss her!" Monica adds loudly.

"Mommy took a vacation. I'm not sure when she'll be back. Now y'all have a good day at school. I better not hear about y'all being bad." Tyrell warns as he drops T.J. and Monica off and watches them run to the teacher.

As he drives away, he begins to talk to God for guidance.

A Love War: TWISTED

"Lord, please help me. I don't know what to do...so many lies for so many years. Forgive me and show me the truth. What am I to do? My best friend betrayed me. My babies' mother and my own wife hate me. I can't sleep, I can't eat. I'm fatigued and emotional. Paying bills by myself now. I hope I get that promotion though."

Suddenly, he sees a car driving into oncoming traffic.

"Hey, this car is driving on the wrong side of the street. Hey! Stop! Move out of the way!" Tyrell exclaims as he blows his horn and swerves.

A Love War: TWISTED

Unknown to Tyrell, Monica is the driver of the car headed towards him. Exhausted from the night before and still intoxicated, she is driving around town almost unaware of her whereabouts, drinking on Jack and Coke.

I haven't stopped drinking since last night. I wonder how Tyrell is. I hope he's alright. Listen to me. I should be worried about my Justin. I don't even know why I married him. Yet for 6 years, he's been my husband...

"I need to lie down. I'm starting to feel dizzy." Monica says to herself.

A Love War: TWISTED

Unaware she is driving on the wrong side of the road, she starts to notice oncoming traffic.

"What's wrong with that car? It barely missed me...why is everyone driving on the wrong side of the street?"

Halfway coherent, Monica finally realizes she is in the wrong lane and starts to swerve.

"Oh shit! Move out of the way!" she screams as she crashes into a oncoming car.

———————————

Meanwhile, Justin is trying to figure out exactly where his head's at and make sense of things.

A Love War: TWISTED

"Man fuck it! I made the bulk of the money anyway! I could outdo Tyrell in anything any day! He always thought he was better than me! But he always amounted to lesser than me... Monica, that bitch! She could have told me. No wonder she cried every night saying to me, "Hold me". This is some fucked up shit. All four of us have problems. She can hold these nuts! Haha! Got em!"

Then Justin thinks of Nicole and her saying she was going to the hospital. *Shining Waters Hospital...I wonder if Nicole is here. I guess I'd better check in. Man I need a beer...*

A Love War: TWISTED

Nicole is in with the doctor, earnestly wanting to go home to get some sleep and forget this whole situation.

"So what is it doctor? Can I go home? Is it just a stomach virus? Something that will move out of my system on its own?"

However, Dr. Collier has other news to tell her.

"Nicole, what have you been doing lately? Are you eating healthy? You need to for the baby.

"Confused and distraught, Nicole's jaw drops and she exclaims. "Excuse me!?! What baby!?! What are you telling me!?!"

Dr. Collier continues. "I am telling you exactly what the tests are telling me. I don't know if it's good news or bad news for you, but I'm afraid you have to take it. You're too far along for an abortion... Nicole, you're pregnant."

Nicole faints.

Tyrell and Monica are both taken to Shining Waters Hospital where Nicole is called and informed of the accident due to Tyrell being her husband.

A Love War: TWISTED

Chapter 6: The Question

Awakening from a deep sleep, high on sedatives from pain, Monica looks around and does not know exactly where she is or how she got there.

What happened? Where am I? Damn, I am sore as fuck...

Doctor Lanberry, comes into the room to check on Monica. Noticing she is awake, he begins to explain the situation.

"Hello Monica. I must say you are blessed or if you're not Christian you're in luck. No broken bones. Just a really bad concussion from the accident. I have to ask you though, do you remember what happened? There are a couple of things I have to tell the police, so please don't get hysterical...cooperate please."

Monica gets hysterical anyway.

"The police!?! What did I do? Why do they need to see me!?!"

"There was alcohol in your system and also traces of THC. Otherwise, I would blame it on fatigue, but you almost killed someone last night. He could barely breathe when he was brought in," Doctor Lanberry explains.

"Who did I hit!?! What's his name? What the hell..." Monica asks with a heavy and fast-paced heart.

A Love War: TWISTED

Doctor Lanberry breaks the news to Monica. "I hate to tell you, but... it was your two kid's father Tyrell...."

An Officer steps into the room after Doctor Lanberry's statement and begins to tell Monica what is about to happen to her.

"That's right ma'am, and now we have to take it a step further. You will be going to jail when you leave the hospital for drunk and reckless driving and maybe attempted murder. We have his story also and we see that you argued the night before. Would that have anything to do with you trying to settle the score?"

"I would never do that! I just made a bad decision. Please don't do this to me.

A Love War: TWISTED

What happens to my kids then!?!" Monica asks as her heart drops and she starts to tear up.

The officer explains.

"They are down at the station since school is over for today. They will be home taken care of by Tyrell's wife until he is okay."

Doctor Lanberry chimes in,.

"Well officer, we have another problem...Nicole is also here, but she will be released soon."

"What is she doing here!?!" Monica exclaims.

Doctor Lanberry pauses, "Well...."

A Love War: TWISTED

Meanwhile, Nicole is talking to Doctor Collier about her situation and her new pregnancy

"Doc I can't do this...I can't do this...I can't do this!!!!"

"Calm down Nicole," says Doctor Collier in a calm voice. "I promise you will get through this. But I have more news, Tyrell was in an accident. The police will take you home soon and tell you what happened."

Nicole shouts!

"Oh my gosh!!! Is he okay! Who was he hit by!?! Where is my bae!?!"

Doctor Collier again tries to calm Nicole.

A Love War: TWISTED

"Calm down. He's stable, just a couple of broken ribs the doctor told me. But I have one more thing to tell you...."

Figuring things could not get much worse, "Come on doc...lay it on me." Nicole says.

Doctor Collier tries to make it sound as nice as he can to deliver the bad news.

"I don't know what's going on with you or how much love you have made or to who...but get your partners checked...when I checked your blood work...you tested positive for HIV/AIDS."

Nicole instantly throws up and shrieks.

A Love War: TWISTED

"What!?! This can't be happening! I only had one affair! This isn't fair! This isn't happening!"

Justin walks into the door with flowers and a concerned face.

"Nicole! I just came by to see if you were okay. The nurse at the desk said you were leaving today. I'll take you home if you want. If that's okay."

"Fuck you, you bastard," Nicole screams.

"Leave me alone okay!?! Fuck you, the situation and the time invested. Oh yeah, I forgot...thanks for the AIDS. Get tested!!!"

Justin is in awe.

A Love War: TWISTED

"Oh shit! You have AIDS!?! Why didn't you tell me?"

Nicole replies, "I had to get it from you! The doctor is just telling me! Now who did you get it from!?! Our baby may have it!"

Justin's jaw drops along with his heart. "Our baby!?!"

Nicole assures.

"Yes, our baby! I'm pregnant too you bastard!"

Unsure and nervous, Justin asks Nicole, "How the fuck do you know it's mine and not Tyrell's?"

"I wasn't fucking Tyrell..." Nicole answers.

A Love War: TWISTED

Justin faints after saying, "I need a doctor. What the hell..."

"God, I'm sorry." Tyrell says. "I've made such a mess, but bless my kids that their kids may be blessed. I know I am not the best of fathers, but I won't be around forever to be a bother."

"Are you ready sir?" The officer asks Tyrell. "It's time to take you home."

Tyrell replies.

"Yes sir. Thank you. Will my kids be home?"

"Yes sir," the officer responds. "Your wife will take care of them until you're better."

A Love War: TWISTED

Without hesitation, Tyrell tells the officer.

"No sir, I request for them to go to their grandmother. My mom doesn't mind. We talked a little while ago."

"Is she able-bodied and capable of taking them where they need to go?" the officer asks.

Tyrell replies, "Yes sir...she keeps them often."

"Okay, well, I don't see a different then. Permission granted."

"Thank you sir, but what happens to Monica?" Tyrell asks in anticipation of a bad result.

A Love War: TWISTED

The officer responds quietly. "She is going to the slammer until you all meet in court to settle things..."

A Love War: TWISTED

Chapter 7: Unexpected Event

Confused, the officer repeats Tyrell's back to him.

"So let me get this straight...you are dropping the charges? Do you realize she can fight for custody?"

Sounding confident Tyrell says, "Come on officer. Hardly. She is already in jail and she hit me. She was drunk I might add. It didn't help I was fatigued."

Intuitive, the officer asks, "So what made you drop the charges? Did she seek legal aid?"

Tyrell pauses and speaks.

"Speaking of aids, that's the reason...I have full-blown AIDS."

A Love War: TWISTED

"Holy shit! You have to be kidding me!?!" The officers exclaims in surprise and shock.

"I was told I don't have long to live you see and the accident made me realize I need to cherish every moment. Instead of making her suffer, I'm using the accident as a good omen." Tyrell says.

The officer sighs and says, "You're better than me..."

Tyrell replies, "I know it...."

Nicole comes in escorted by police after they knock and asks...

"Hey...how are you feeling...I have some news for you... I'm pregnant...and I have AIDS, but know that I love you...."

A Love War: TWISTED

Tyrell is in shock.

"What!?! How!?! We never did anything!?! Is it Justin's?"

"Yes," Nicole replies.

Tyrell sighs.

"Oh, so he is the one who is going to make you suffer..."

"What do you mean?" Nicole asks

Tyrell informs Nicole of his last secret.

"One last secret baby...I have AIDS too. That is my reason for never sleeping with you. But if Justin has it and he's married to Monica..."

Nicole asks in anticipation, "Wait! Who did you get it from!?!"

A Love War: TWISTED

"Monica...." Tyrell replies in shame.

Nicole throws her hands up and shouts, "Lord, have mercy! The drama!!!"

"Should we leave?" The officers ask.

"Hell yes!" Tyrell and Nicole shout simultaneously.

The officers leave in haste, relieved to be away from the scene of such drama.

"So what now!?!" Nicole asks. "I'm so over this! I wanna fight!"

"Listen, we were all wrong...so let's all try to make this right." Tyrell says, trying to alleviate any stress over the situation.

"I called Justin. He will be here soon. We made amends over the phone but we should face to face too. I also posted Monica's bail. She will also be here soon. So what do you think Nicole? We all start over and call it truce?"

Justin knocks and walks in and chimes in on the conversation.

"We can call it truce man, but what about the kids?"

Tyrell replies, "We will all play a role just like my grandparents and parents did. This doesn't have to end as a bad experience."

"You're right, it doesn't, but look at what Monica's freedom did to her..."

The reporter on the news is speaking,

A Love War: TWISTED

"32 year old-black female dead on arrival after being accidentally hit by a car. She was said to be jumping for joy in the street when the car hit her."

"I'm so bitter..." Justin says.

"We all are, but what can we do?" Tyrell replies.

Justin says in a slow and sad voice,

"I know what she would have wanted. Let's call it truce."

Nicole, Justin and Tyrell all agree to a truce.

Tyrell tries to change the mood by changing the subject.

A Love War: TWISTED

"We will talk about funeral arrangements later. Let's go get the kids. Mom is doing me a huge favor."

"I can't believe she's gone," Nicole says distraughtly

Tyrell puts his hand on Nicole's shoulder as he says.

"Mourn for a while. But the best thing you can do is be a mother to her children"

"But you're still here. What does that make me? Nothing?" Justin asks in despair and wonder.

Tyrell reassures Justin.

A Love War: TWISTED

"You are very much a part of this too, "Uncle Justin". Now let's get the kids before my mom kills me."

Starting to feel better, Nicole replies "I love you guys."

Justin and Tyrell respond simultaneously,

"We know. You told us both!"

With attitude Nicole exclaims, "Really!?!"

Justin replies, "You know we were just playing girl. Lighten up."

Nicole tells Justin.

"I'm going to stick my foot in your ass!"

A Love War: TWISTED

Tyrell tries to take control of the situation.

"All right! That's enough! I thought we were going to get the children. I didn't know they were already here!

Ten

Years

Later

A Love War: TWISTED

Chapter 8: T.J.'s Incident

"God...who am I? Who are you? I was told you created me. But, why would you create me to go through so much hell? I'm on a journey to find myself and find you. They say you know everything, but I thought I would tell you this...my daddy gone kill me when he finds out I skipped school. I hope Monica doesn't tell."

T.J., now in high school, has reached a pivotal point in life and doesn't know where to turn. Times like this he really missed Nicole being with them. She was the nurturer in his life, so lenient and full of compassion, unlike his strict father. He now spends most of his time with the wrong crowd and smoking weed.

At home, Tyrell is concerned because T.J. hasn't made it home from school yet and it's close to dinnertime. Justin and Nicole would be over soon.

"Monica, where is your brother? And don't tell me you don't know, y'all stick together harder than overcooked rice in a pan."

"Well daddy, he was on the bus this morning, but afterwards, I didn't see him anymore. When he didn't get on the bus after school, I figured he was staying late to watch Candace practice. You know he does that sometimes."

A Love War: TWISTED

"Watch Candace practice or watch Candace in general? That boy isn't head over heels, he's head on heels! Bending over backwards for that girl. He got it honest though."

"What do you mean he got it honest daddy? Who did you bend over backwards for?"

"Baby, that's not important." Tyrell said, not wanting her to know that he would bend over backwards for her biological mother, Monica. T.J. and Monica grew up with Nicole as their mother until she and Tyrell divorced and she went to be with Justin. They were too young to remember

Monica and for now, he wanted to keep it that way.

"Well, how important am I to you?"

"What the hell is that supposed to mean?" Tyrell didn't know where this conversation was going nor did he like it.

"I was just asking because I haven't been feeling very loved lately, but if you bought me that Michael Kors purse we saw at the mall yesterday I would."

Tyrell knew that Monica had officially lost her mind. Where was this sense of entitlement coming from?

"Three questions...What job do you have; how would it benefit you and since I already know the answer to question one, do you plan on getting a job soon to pay me back the $300 for it?"

"Never mind…I'll just ask Uncle Justin or Aunt Nicole. Collectively all three of you can contribute $100 for me!"

"Girl, go set the table while I try to find your brother. Uncle Justin and Aunt Nicole will be over so set them a place too." Raising teenagers as a single father is definitely a challenge.

Monica, not the one to give up so easily, decided to make one last attempt at persuading her dad.

"What if I pay for it by working around the house?"

A Love War: TWISTED

Irritated, Tyrell yelled, "Go do what I said!"

"It was worth a shot...." She said under her breath.

As Monica was going to set the table, there was a knock at the door.

"They're mad early...." Tyrell said expecting it to be Justin and Nicole at the door. To his surprise, it was a police officer instead.

"Hello sir, how are you this evening?" The officer greeted him.

"I am well officer. What can I help you with?"

A Love War: TWISTED

"I found an ID in an alley with this address. I was returning it. Is the boy home?"

"No, he's not. I was just going to look for him."

"How long has he been missing?"

"I haven't seen him since this morning when he got on the bus." Tyrell explained.

"Don't worry sir. Boys of this age just like girls do this all of the time. I am sure it's nothing and he will be home soon. I will be looking in the vicinity and put out an APB to bring him home."

A Love War: TWISTED

"Thank you officer. I really appreciate it." Tyrell closed the door and went into the dining room.

"Who was that daddy?" Monica asked hoping it was T.J..

"Is the table set sweetheart?" Tyrell said, changing the subject.

"Yea, did you find T.J.?"

"Baby, go call Uncle Justin and Aunt Nicole and see if they are on their way." He requested of her, avoiding the question.

"But what about…?"

"Sweetie, just do what I said okay?" Worried about T.J. and his whereabouts, Tyrell didn't see the need to make Monica worried too. When she was out of the room he thought aloud,

"Son, please come home. I hope you're okay...."

Chapter 9: Disrupted Dinner

The doorbell rang shortly after Monica hung up the phone with Justin. Hoping it was T.J. or Justin and Nicole as opposed to some bad news, Tyrell hesitantly opened the door.

Upon opening the door he saw that it was Justin and Nicole.

"Hey guys! How's everything?" He said relieved, that it wasn't another police officer, but disappointed that it wasn't T.J.

Noticing how out of character Tyrell was acting, Justin said,

"What's wrong man?"

"What do you mean?" Tyrell said.

A Love War: TWISTED

"Usually, by now you would have started talking shit and trying to kick us out before we even get in the door." Nicole replied, noticing how strange he was acting as well.

Laughing, Tyrell says "Oh damn... Am I that mean? It's just that T.J. isn't home yet and a cop found his ID in an alley."

"He probably dropped it while he was with some friends man. He'll turn up, and so will we!" Justin said, revealing the bottle of Cîroc he was holding behind his back.

"Why are we turning up on a Wednesday man?" Tyrell asked curiously.

A Love War: TWISTED

"Yes, do tell...." Nicole was also curious to know what his response would be.

Laughing, Justin said.

"The youngins got the club goin' up on a Tuesday, so I'm turnin' up on a Wednesday!"

"Not funny Uncle Justin!" Monica said, shaking her head at Justin trying to sound hip.

"I tried...Man what's for dinner?"

"Deez nuts!" Tyrell answered jokingly; trying to sound hip as well.

"Daddy!" Monica exclaimed, embarrassed at how her dad and Justin were acting.

"Had to get 'em!" He replied.

A Love War: TWISTED

"Well then, now that the teenager is out of everyone's system, even though there is only one in the house, can we gather round for prayer?" Nicole said, trying to get everyone's attention back on the reason they were gathered.

As they were walking into the dining room Tyrell replied, "Just a little fun…keeps you young sweetheart."

"Your sweetheart is…?" Nicole retorted.

"So how about that prayer Nicole?" Justin said seeing that Nicole was becoming riled and ready to go off on Tyrell.

A Love War: TWISTED

Before Nicole could say anything else, Tyrell asked that everyone grab hands and close their eyes as he began to pray,

"Dear Lord, we thank you for our fellowship here this evening. We pray that the food prepared be physical nourishment to our bodies. And father...wherever my son is...let our love reach him and point him in the direction of home very soon. Thank you Lord for all of these blessing now..."

"Amen! Let's eat!" Justin said cutting, Tyrell's prayer short.

"Rudeness!!!" Nicole yelled.

A Love War: TWISTED

Just as Nicole and Justin began to bicker, Monica yelled for Tyrell in the living room.

"Daddy somebody is on the phone for you!"

"Hello." Tyrell said hoping T.J. was on the other end of the phone. Unfortunately it is Doctor Eisenhower.

"Hello, is this Mr. Tyrell Weston?"

"Yes it is. What can I do for you doc?" Tyrell said coughing; knowing the reason for this call couldn't be good.

"We have your son here at the hospital running some tests. He is stable, but I recommend he stay the night. We need a parent or guardian here to stay with him."

A Love War: TWISTED

At a loss for words, Tyrell just held the phone silently crying. He didn't know how bad things were for T.J., but if his son needed to stay at the hospital overnight he knew his condition couldn't be too good.

"Mr. Weston?" Dr. Eisenhower said, breaking into Tyrell's silence.

"Do you know what happened to him? Where was he found?" To give him a little peace, Tyrell needed to know all the details the doctor could provide to him over the phone.

Unfortunately the doctor couldn't tell him anything. He just advised him to speak to the officer once he got there.

A Love War: TWISTED

"The police officer who found him is here at the hospital to answer all of the questions you have." Dr. Eisenhower replied.

Before hanging up, Tyrell said, "Thank you doc. I'm on my way."

After talking to Dr. Eisenhower, Tyrell joined Justin, Nicole and Monica back in the dining room. Sensing something was wrong Justin said,

"What's up man? You good?" and Monica followed up with "Daddy what's wrong?"

Tyrell didn't have time to answer any questions. He needed to get to his son.

A Love War: TWISTED

"Monica put on your shoes. Nicole, Justin...if you want to go we are going to see T.J. at the hospital."

Sensing the urgency in his voice Nicole said, "Oh my gosh! What happened?"

"We don't know yet."

Thinking only of himself, Justin said "Can we eat first? I mean he ain't goin' nowhere..."

Hearing the selfish words come out of Justin's mouth pissed Nicole off.

"You selfish bastard! I swear you... See that's why I..." She was so upset with him she couldn't even get her thoughts together to finish the sentence.

A Love War: TWISTED

T.J. was in the hospital, possibly fighting for his life, and all Justin could think of was food. How would he have felt if it were his son in the hospital and Tyrell had a nonchalant attitude? Justin could be such an asshole. She loved him so much, but sometimes his attitude made her wonder why. What did she see in him in the first place to make her decide she wanted to be with him over Tyrell?

Tyrell interrupted her thoughts, "Are you guys coming or not...?"

"I'll drive." She said.

Alright y'all....Let's pray along the way.

A Love War: TWISTED

Chapter 10: The Scare, The Wonder

Arriving at the hospital in less than fifteen minutes, Tyrell, Justin, Nicole and Monica all went to the receptionist desk to see which room T.J. was in.

After being given the room number, they all went in, relieved to see that he was alert. Tyrell was the first to speak to his son.

"Hey son, how are you feeling? I know you were probably expecting me to be mad at you or yell, but your well-being is my only concern at the moment. What did the doctors say?"

"They said I passed out because of a scratch I have. I lost a lot of blood. They said something about cap pistols or something not closing the hole up. I'm like I have no idea what they're talking about…"

Monica couldn't help but interrupt the conversation to correct her brother.

"It's capillaries big brother… Lord, have mercy."

At that time, Dr. Eisenhower walked in and interrupted the family moment.

"I'm sorry folks, there's only two visitors at a time." He said.

Being the pain in the rear end he couldn't help but be, Justin said,

"Brother we ain't visitors, we family. Ya dig?"

A Love War: TWISTED

Irritated Nicole said, "Get yourself out here in the waiting room with me and stop being an ass!"

As Justin and Nicole walked out, Tyrell pulled Dr. Eisenhower off to the side, "Doc, I need to speak with you in private about something."

"Of course, of course."

"Have you run any tests on him?"

"We have run all of the tests we need to run. Everything checks out normal. It's just that the cut was deeper than the usual cut that's all."

"I was asking because, well...you know my condition and the condition his mother had…"

A Love War: TWISTED

"I am aware and just like I told you long ago, there are no signs of it on our screenings of him or Monica. I assure you there is nothing to worry about."

Just as Tyrell and Dr. Eisenhower finished their conversation, T.J. looked at Tyrell and said, "Dad, I need to talk to you when we get home."

"Okay, when they release you and everything checks out we will talk at home okay? For now just enjoy that bed I have to pay for."

"I'm sorry..." T.J. Said, not being able to help but feel bad about the situation he has gotten himself into and the worry he was causing his dad. The incident had also left him with some questions he felt only Tyrell could answer.

"Now isn't the time. We will talk about it later."

"Daddy, I'm hungry. We should go get something to eat." Monica said.

"Soon baby." He replied.

Meanwhile in the waiting room, Nicole and Justin are having a heated discussion that leads to Nicole being in tears.

"Why the hell do you always have to do this when we go out to places?" Nicole asked.

"Would you rather me be anyone but me? Isn't that who you told me to be when you met me?"

A Love War: TWISTED

"Look, let's not go back in the past, that's why I've been snapping lately. It's just...I see how Monica and T.J. are growing and...I mean...what if I didn't miscarry? I could have had one of my own right now."

"Listen, everything happens for a reason okay? Obviously God was telling you then wasn't the time and he was telling me I wasn't ready for a child because Lord knows I'm immature!"

At that statement, Nicole couldn't help but laugh because he was definitely telling the truth, the whole truth and nothing but the truth. He *is* undeniably immature.

"This isn't supposed to be funny!" She said.

A Love War: TWISTED

With a smile, Justin commented.

"Life is nothing if you don't find moments that make you smile. Why can't it be every moment? That's why I joke so much. All jokes aside, I wonder too, but all we can do is move on and thank God we are still living."

"I guess you're right..."

"Why are they taking him out in a wheelchair? He can walk!" Monica asked upset.

"So the hospital doesn't get sued sweetie, it's protocol." Tyrell explained.

"Well put me in a wheelchair too!" Monica said dramatically.

Rolling his eyes, Tyrell said

A Love War: TWISTED

"Girl, get in the car and stop being messy now! Everybody ready?"

"Yes, I'm ready." Nicole said sniffing and drying her tears.

"Y'all two okay over there? Is it Justin's breath again Nicole?"

"Very funny...Nah, she cried because it's sad how ugly you are." Justin countered.

"Ha-ha, alright I'll give you that. We got dinner warming. Y'all still coming to eat?"

"Yea, I'm hungry." Nicole said.

As they were walking out of the hospital to head back to Tyrell's house, Justin walked ahead of Nicole to walk next to Tyrell and said.

A Love War: TWISTED

"Ty, I need to talk to you later on man."

"Alright, cool. Let's get out of here." He replied.

A Love War: TWISTED

Chapter 11: The Return

As soon as everyone walked into the house T.J. pulled Tyrell off to the side. He really wanted to talk to him about what happened to him before he ended up in the hospital. He really needed to get the incident off his chest and get some clarification on some things.

"Dad, I really need to get this off my chest."

"We will talk after dinner, now go wash up. It's already late."

"Daddy, do you want me to warm the hen up in the oven?" Monica asked.

"Yes, for about 10 minutes okay? Nicole, can you help her please? You remember what happened last time we left that girl in the kitchen?"

"Um...yea, I'll be right there." Nicole said, remembering what happened that day.

As T.J. left the room to go wash up and Monica went into the kitchen, Tyrell called Nicole back feeling the need to check on her.

"Hey, you okay? You've been acting strange ever since we left the hospital. Everything alright?"

"Yea, I'm fine. I was just thinking on some things..." She said with hesitation.

Knowing what was on her mind, Justin interrupted.

"Yo bro, how about that talk?"

"After dinner. T.J. said he wants to talk too, so right after that. Alright, everybody ready for dinner? Moni, go get your brother out of the bathroom please."

"T.J.! Daddy said come on. It's time to eat!" Monica yelled.

Shaking his head, he said aloud to God.

"God, I know you said be specific when I ask you for things, but I didn't think I had to be specific when I tell my kids to do something..." he then turned and stated to Monica.

A Love War: TWISTED

"Monica I could have done that. I specifically said go get your brother out of the bathroom."

"And I did daddy… See, there he go."

"The point is I told you to go get him... that involves movement."

"My voice carried daddy, so I moved since it was my voice."

Annoyed by his daughter's smart mouth, Tyrell said.

"I will deal with you later. Grace has been said. Let's eat."

At the dinner table, everyone except T.J. begins to fix a plate. Not paying much attention to how zoned out T.J. Is, Nicole says,

"T.J., could you pass the potatoes please?"

Due to the incident being on his mind he did not hear her. He just sat staring off into space.

"Son, please pass Nicole the potatoes." Tyrell said.

Continuing to stare off into space in a daze, T.J. heard nothing and made no movement.

"T.J....?" Tyrell said, now more concerned than ever, but T.J. continued to sit there as if in a state of unconsciousness.

A Love War: TWISTED

"T.J.!" Tyrell yelled, hoping to get T.J.'s attention. If he didn't respond soon, Tyrell would have to take him back to the hospital. Fortunately, this time, Tyrell got a response.

"Sir?" T.J. said as he jumped; startled back into reality.

Knowing the talk between he and his son couldn't wait a second longer, he said,

Please excuse us y'all." He stood up from the table and said to T.J.,

"In the kitchen. Now."

When they entered the kitchen, T.J. said, "I'm sorry."

Concerned and irritated, Tyrell yelled,

A Love War: TWISTED

"What's wrong with you!?! What the hell is going on!?!"

"That's what I wanted to talk to you about. I didn't scrape myself or anything. Somebody cut my wrist...."

"I told you about messing with those boys smoking and crap!"

Tyrell felt him hanging with the wrong crowd is what caused this whole mess, but he had no idea what was about to transpire.

"No, it wasn't them. I was alone. It was a lady. She put something over my mouth and nose and I blacked out after she did it."

A Love War: TWISTED

T.J. began to explain why he didn't make it home after school and what landed him in the hospital. As he was explaining, the conversation was interrupted by yelling in the dining room.

"Well I don't give a damn about what you have accomplished! I'm talking about now!" Nicole yelled.

"Well fuck you! I turned my life around for you and this how you treat me!?!" Justin shouted.

Tyrell left T.J. in the kitchen to see what was going on.

"Hey! What the hell is going on in here!?!"

A Love War: TWISTED

"I'm sorry bro, I gotta go!" Justin said, fuming as he walked towards the door to leave.

"But I thought you wanted to talk?"

"No reason to now! I wouldn't have a baby with her if my life depended on it!"

Just as Justin was about to walk out the door, there was a knock.

"Who the fuck is it!?! There's nobody home." He yelled as he opened the door.

When he opened it, he saw a handwritten letter on the porch.

"Who the fuck delivers mail at night? Bro, this is for you though." He said as he hands Tyrell the letter.

A Love War: TWISTED

"Oh my god..." Tyrell says as he recognizes the handwriting on the letter.

"What is it daddy?" Monica asks.

Not believing his eyes, Tyrell just simply said,

"Kids go get ready for bed, I need to talk to Nicole and Justin alone."

Still needing to finish his conversation with Tyrell, T.J. says "But dad what about…?"

Tyrell cuts him off and says,

"We will talk about more tomorrow, okay."

He then turns his attention to Justin and Nicole and says,

"Guys...sit down…"

A Love War: TWISTED

Sensing the nervousness in Tyrell's voice, Nicole says,

"What's going on? Who's that letter from?"

"Yea man, c'mon. You have me scared as hell right now." Justin said worried.

"Y'all I hope someone is playing with me. This letter is from..."

"Who?"

Justin asked as Tyrell just stood there not able to finish his sentence.

"Yea, who?" Nicole asked anxiously.

Tyrell couldn't believe his eyes and he didn't know how to say it. How would he tell them that he has just received a letter from the grave?

A Love War: TWISTED

He finally found the strength and courage to say, "Monica..."

A Love War: TWISTED

Chapter 12: The Game Begins

In shock from the letter he has just received, Tyrell has a flash back to the day his children's mother, Monica, was killed by a car.

"32 year-old black female dead on arrival to the hospital after she was accidentally hit by a car. She was said to be jumping for joy in the street when the car hit her..." were the words he remembers the reporter saying.

"It can't be... It just can't." Tyrell manages to utter.

"Well, what does the letter say?" Nicole asks apprehensively.

A Love War: TWISTED

Tyrell reads the letter aloud for both Nicole and Justin to hear,

"To my sweet and wonderful Ty: I am back from the dead or so it seems. It's funny what you can do with money isn't it? Especially when you have so much of it that almost anyone or anything seems to have a price. Yet, the one we have all paid is something even money can't fix.

Tell Justin I said fuck him just like I know he's still fucking Nicole, though legally he's still married to me. I got my half for the divorce. Maybe he should do the same. Also, tell Nicole I'm sorry about the miscarriage. Everyone isn't meant to be a mother. And you sir...I'm going to get

right to the point... I WANT MY KIDS.
You selfish bastard! You know the only
reason you even had them to begin with
was because I was unstable. You agreed to
give them back and I want them. All you
have to do is meet me at the courthouse to
settle this. I have an email you can reach
me at engraved at the bottom. I hope to
hear from you soon."

devil'sdaughter@gmail.com

"P.S. Don't even think about trying
to find me before we meet. I don't go by
Monica anymore."

After reading the letter, Tyrell, Justin
and Nicole all stand frozen in place unable
to speak. They couldn't believe Monica was

alive after all this time. They all wondered how she knew about Nicole's miscarriage. They also wondered how she now looks. They all knew she had to have gotten cosmetic surgery because there is no way she could still look the same and no one had spotted her.

Tyrell was the first to speak.

"There's no way in hell she's taking my kids away from me!"

"Fuck that! That bitch said I can't be a mother!?! I swear we gon' find her!" Nicole stated, obviously outraged and offended.

A Love War: TWISTED

"So... I'm still married yo... But how does she know all of this?" Justin said, shaking his head in disbelief.

"I don't know, but I am sure as hell going to find out..." Tyrell said.

Around the corner, T.J. and Monica are eavesdropping on the conversation taking place between their father, Nicole and Justin.

"Damn..."

"T.J.!" Monica yelled at T.J.'s word choice.

"I'm sorry, but you know what this means...?"

A Love War: TWISTED

"Not exactly...who is Monica?" Monica asked, unaware of whom her biological mother actually was.

"Monica is our mom. That's why dad never wanted to talk about her. She supposedly died years ago when we were younger. He told me not to tell you because he didn't feel you were ready."

"So I guess you thought I was just now...?"

"Well, now we know she's not dead and I bet that's the woman..."

"What T.J.?" Monica asked, unaware of where the conversation she and her brother were having was headed.

A Love War: TWISTED

"Well…this cut on my wrist is in the shape of an "M"." T.J. Said, beginning to explain to her the events of the incident that landed him in the hospital hours earlier.

"Wait... you think mom cut you!?!" Monica asked, confused about why their own mother would hurt him.

"Come on, let's go to your room and talk before we get caught. I can't believe this..."

Back in the living room, Tyrell, Justin and Nicole are still in shocked disbelief over the letter.

"I can't believe this..." Tyrell says.

A Love War: TWISTED

"Hell none of us can... So she just wants the kids? Just give her visitation rights man... The kids are almost grown now anyway, but why of all times does she want to be in their lives?"

Coughing, Tyrell says, "I can't be entirely sure man. As much as it hurts me to do...I am going to have to go to war with her on this one..."

"Ty, just try to come to a compromise via email first, then if she doesn't want to hear it, do what you have to do." Nicole suggested.

"I just think this is deeper than the kids..." Tyrell said.

A Love War: TWISTED

"What happened was years ago, do you really think she held on all of this time?" Justin asked.

"Dude, you heard the letter! She is back with a vengeance! We all have to watch our backs... Look guys, I'm tired. I need some time with God before I go to bed." Tyrell said, drained from T.J.'s earlier incident and now this letter from **"the woman formally known to them as Monica"**.

"Guess that's our cue to leave. Alright boo, goodnight." Nicole says, as she and Justin walked towards the door.

"Alright man, call us if you need anything." Justin said.

A Love War: TWISTED

"Will do."

After Justin and Nicole leave, Tyrell kneels next to his bed for prayer.

"Our Father who art in heaven, hallowed by thy name... Lord, I need you. I don't know what the future holds, but I know that you are God and nothing is impossible with you. I need you now in this situation more than ever. I am scared. I am afraid of losing my kids. I am afraid of losing it all. Keep me Lord. Don't let me fall by the wayside because of the past. Have mercy on me through this and let me be victorious in the end. In your name I proclaim victory. Amen."

A Love War: TWISTED

As Tyrell arises from his knees confident in knowing that God would take care of the situation he was in, he pulls back the covers on his bed.

"Oh my god!" He yelled.

Hearing him, T.J. and Monica run into the room.

"Dad what's wrong!?!" T.J. asked.

"What happened!?! Is that a snake!?! Omg!!!!" Monica screamed hysterically.

"T.J., take your sister to your room, now!" Tyrell demanded.

As T.J. takes Monica to his room, Tyrell reads the note left on his bed next to the snake.

A Love War: TWISTED

"I hope you like my symbols. I am going to expose you for the snake you are then let time kill you. I will have my kids one way or another. "

Signed,

The Devil's Daughter

A Love War: TWISTED

Chapter 13: The Charge

Look at me....I have so much, but I have nothing. Gained everything and lost nothing... Tyrell... that bastard. Took everything from me! Didn't want to be with me!?! Wanted Nicole!?! And now he makes it seem like he has no one!?! Well, I have a little surprise for him... Monica, the mother of Tyrell's children has something in store for him and he better be ready.

On the other side of town, Tyrell is at home thinking of the events of the night before and his phone rings abruptly breaking him of his train of thought. A smile comes across his face when he sees that it's Desiree, a woman he met about a year ago at a restaurant called Ladonna's, which is around the corner from Johnson Pharmaceuticals where he works.

"Hello?"

"Hey sexy, what going on? What are you doing?" Desiree says in a sexy, seductive tone.

"Relaxing while the kids are at school. What's up?"

"I was trying to see you if I could after work. I was going to work out and then work you out if you know what I mean." Desiree answered, still in a sexy seductive way.

"Sweetheart, can we make this for another time? I want to spend time with my kids, unless you think it's time for y'all to meet."

"Isn't that what I have been begging you for?"

"Well, how about you come to dinner tonight? We are going to Schavelli's on Bradley Ave. Say, meet us there at 7:00 so I can introduce you?"

"Yes, that sounds perfect. I'm so excited! See you all then!" Desiree said.

"Alright bae. Bye."

Later that night, Desiree leaves her home to head to Schavelli's to meet Tyrell, Monica and T.J.. She wanted to go to a store first to buy a little something for Tyrell's children with the hopes they would like her.

A Love War: TWISTED

Little did she know, she would not make it to the store or Schavelli's. She was grabbed by a hooded figured and drug into an alley.

Meanwhile at home, Tyrell is waiting for Monica and T.J. to finish getting dressed so they could leave.

"Kids! Are you ready? We're going to be late!"

"Dad how are we going to be late when it's just us?" T.J. didn't know Tyrell has a woman in his life that he wanted them to meet.

"I have something for you all to see."

Monica, being the smart-aleck she always is said,

A Love War: TWISTED

"Did you get me a car finally!?!"

"Yea, a hot wheels." Tyrell said sarcastically.

"Now I see where I get my smart mouth from."

"Yea, your mother, but let's go." Tyrell says as they leave to head to the restaurant.

After Tyrell, T.J. and Monica arrive and are seated at Schavelli's they are greeted by their waiter.

"Good Evening, my name is Chad; I will be your waiter for this evening. What can I get you all to drink?"

"Can I get a sprite?"

"May I have a coke?"

A Love War: TWISTED

"May I have water please?" Monica, T.J. and Tyrell all reply respectively.

"Sprite, coke and water, got it. Be right back." The waiter says as he leaves to get their drinks.

"So where is our surprise daddy?" Monica asks.

Pulling out his phone, Tyrell replies, "I haven't gotten a response..."

Infuriated, T.J. yells, "So it's a woman!?! Man I'm gone!"

Running after T.J., Tyrell pleads, "T.J., wait! Son! Talk to me!"

Once Tyrell has caught up with T.J. he begins to explain how he's feeling.

A Love War: TWISTED

"T.J., I have been lonely for years okay. Ever since the situation happened years ago, I have done nothing but raise you guys, but what happens after y'all go to college? I'll be alone. I just want you guys to meet the woman who is going to keep me company and I hope to marry one day. Son, no one can ever replace your mother, but I can't sit and grieve for the rest of my life either. Please son, give me this much at least."

"Okay, I'm sorry dad. It's just....we never knew her and you never wanted to talk about her."

"How about tomorrow when you all get out of school?"

A Love War: TWISTED

"So, y'all just gone leave me siting at the table? Rude! Our food is here!" Monica says sourly when she comes outside to see her dad and brother having a father-son moment.

"Baby, we didn't order anything...." Tyrell said, wondering what food was awaiting them.

When they reenter the restaurant, the waiter says,

"Someone called in a special order for you all. A steak and potatoes on a silver platter."

Regrettably, when the waiter opens the platter, it is not steak and potatoes they see. It is a woman's head and a heart with a note in front of it.

"Oh my god!!!!! Desiree... No..."

"T.J., take your sister to the car okay...." Seeing Desiree like this made him sick to his stomach. He was really hoping to be able to spend a lifetime with her.

He realizes now more than ever that the mother of his children is definitely not playing games. He had to do something and quick before she killed anyone else he loved.

"Daddy...was this who we were supposed to meet...?" T.J. asked.

"Just do what I said okay!!!!" Tyrell yelled.

"Daddy..." Monica said.

A Love War: TWISTED

"Go!!!!" Tyrell yelled again.

"I'm so sorry sir...I'll call the police right away. Again I am so sorry." The waiter said.

As the waiter walks away to call the police, Tyrell picks up the note on the platter, reading it.

"She was so pretty. I see why you chose her. She was a fighter just like you. Nice display of a head and heart isn't it? You can take it home if you like. I would prefer a doggy bag if I were you. I am sorry she was ever involved with you. She really did have a bright future. Metaphor? Oh yea, charge this to my head and not my heart.

A Love War: TWISTED

Monica"

"I'm going to get that bitch if it's the last thing I do!!!..." Tyrell snarls.

A Love War: TWISTED

Chapter 14: Betrayal

As soon as Tyrell and the children arrive back home, Tyrell sends T.J. and Monica to their room and he sits down at his computer and begins to email Monica.

Monica,

Words can't express how I feel. Whatever I did to you I am so sorry. No one had any idea you were alive. Why didn't you just call? Come by? Why did it have to come to this? But I'm going to give you what you want. You have taken so much from me and I should return the favor...but that's not me. All I need from you is the address of the courthouse and a time. I won't even need my lawyer for this...

A Love War: TWISTED

Sincerely,

Tyrell

"God forgive me, for I know not what I am going to do." Tyrell says under his breath. Moments later he receives a reply to his email.

Tyrell,

You're right; you won't need your lawyer. What you will need is to bring the kids with you so they can go home with me. I have something very near and dear to you that I know will make you hand them over to me. Yes, you are sorry; a sorry excuse for a man and a father.

The address you will need to meet me at is 4820 Langley Court. The time is

A Love War: TWISTED

4:00 a.m. TOMORROW. Since it's the weekend, it shouldn't be a problem. See you there.

Signed,

The Devil's Daughter

P.S. Pray for Justin and Nicole.

"I never thought...it...it would come to this." Tyrell says; shedding a tear.

"Dad you okay? What did the police say?" T.J. asks.

"They have to investigate going son. Go get your sister. I need to talk to the both of you."

"What's going on daddy?" Monica asks as she enters the room.

A Love War: TWISTED

"Y'all are my babies, and regardless of how old y'all get...y'all will be my babies." Tyrell sighs knowing the rest of the conversation would not be easy, but he must get everything out in the open so he continues.

"Your mom...Your mom was a sweet woman upon me meeting her. Angelic... Wonderful... Almost perfect. The only thing was...she always wanted things her way and in this world that's not how it works. Now, I am not going to lie to you all and say I did everything right, but one thing I did do was stay faithful to her until we ended. Your aunt Nicole used to be my wife and Uncle Justin used to be married to your mom. You all are too young to remember much. We had a huge fight, all of us, and…it ended in a car crash which is why I get a check now on top of my pay from the job..."

"...Your mom went to jail and I bailed her out, trying to be a good person and she was said to be hit by a car upon release. I thought she was dead. We all did, but...apparently she didn't die. And now she wants to take y'all away from me. I know I have not been the best father or the perfect example of what being grown is and..."

No longer able to suppress his tears, Tyrell begins to cry as he continues.

"I...just hope you can forgive me for the wrongs I have done and the things I have hidden. I just wanted to protect you and I wish none of this would have ever happened. Please forgive me..."

"Dad... I forgive you, but I don't feel you have anything to be sorry for. You have taken care of us from day one, stepped up to the plate like many men don't do. I love and respect you for that."

T.J. Said, trying to show his dad that he understood why he hid everything from them up until now.

"I love you daddy....I always will. You my hero, my rock." Monica added.

"Well, your mom has made a request... She wants me to meet her and bring y'all with me. Are you willing to go?

I promise nothing is going to happen to you."

"When and where daddy?" T.J. asked.

"I'll go daddy. Anything for you." Monica said as she hugged him.

"I don't know exactly where y'all, but we are going to get through this together. Get some sleep now okay? We have to be up early for this..."

"How early?" T.J. and Monica asked simultaneously.

"We have to be there at 4:00." Tyrell replied.

The next morning, Tyrell, T.J. and Monica are up and prepared to leave at 3:00.

A Love War: TWISTED

"Y'all ready to meet your mom?" Tyrell asked; already knowing the answer to the question considering the time of day.

"As I'll ever be at 3:00 in the morning." T.J. said half sleep.

"Momma must've been an early bird. Glad we got all your traits!"

"Girl, get in the car." Tyrell said laughing

When they arrive at address, all they saw was a spooky abandoned factory building. Tyrell doesn't have a clue what he has put his children in the middle of.

"Oh my god..." He says.

"Are you sure this is the right address dad?" T.J. asked uncertainly.

A Love War: TWISTED

"This place is nasty, creepy and dirty... Who's that!?!" Monica says pointing at a hooded figure near a door as it walks in.

"I think you all know who that is... Do you guys want to stay in the car? I'm letting you make your first decision on your own right now." Tyrell said wearily.

"Well, in that case...let's go daddy." T.J. said ready to face his mother.

"I ain't staying in this car by myself so I'm goin' too!"

"Monica! I've done what you asked! Now come on out so we can handle this!" Tyrell demanded. "Stay close to me..." He says to T.J. and Monica, not knowing what their mother had up her sleeve.

A Love War: TWISTED

From the shadows they hear a voice, "It's not Monica anymore... It's Desdemona, because I should have listened to my dad about you!" Desdemona appears; standing face to face with them.

"Is that what this is all about? The lies you told to be with me? Desdemona we were young but look at the blessings that came from it." Tyrell protests as he points to the kids.

Looking at T.J. and Monica, Desdemona sheds a tear, reaches for them and says, "My... children..."

"Don't you dare touch them!" Tyrell says as he steps in front of them protecting them from whatever Desdemona may try to do.

"Give me my kids! Or..."Desdemona says as she flips a light switch to reveal Nicole and Justin tied down laying over a pit of battery acid with a blade ready to swing back and forth over them.

"Their lives are in your hands Tyrell... Nicole is already critical. Figured you would care more for her than Justin. So what is it going to be "Mr. I have all the answers"?"

"You're a sick bitch..." Tyrell says as he sees his friends whose lives are in danger. He couldn't believe the woman he once loved was capable of these acts.

A Love War: TWISTED

"And my kids are the cure!" Desdemona says as she runs to the top of the stairs with Tyrell close behind her.

"Dad!" T.J. yells.

"T.J., I need you to be strong for me okay? Protect your sister." Tyrell instructed T.J..

"Mommy will be there soon sweethearts!" Desdemona says to T.J. and Monica.

"So what's your decision? I push this red button they die. I push this blue button, they live with minor injuries." She states to Tyrell.

"So either way, I make the decision to inflict pain on them…?"

A Love War: TWISTED

"Them being paralyzed won't be so bad."

"Why are you doing this!?!"

"Because you never listened to me! You never wanted me! Then you marry my best friend!?!"

"Hell, you married my best friend! It's called life woman! Things happen that we can't control! We are only in control of our own actions! Look at our kids, crying! Scared! Is that what you want!?! Look at those whom you once loved! One in critical condition and the other scared out of his mind! And it all boils down to us! If you want revenge take it out on me! Hurt me!

A Love War: TWISTED

Kill me! But let them go! None of them deserve this!"

Crying harder and stepping towards the edge of the pit, Desdemona says.

"I wish you'd loved me the way you loved everyone else... You know, we never got a chance to get married, but I said I would always love you 'til death did us part." After saying that she steps even closer to the edge.

"Des, don't do this…" Tyrell pleads.

"Take this ring... The last I have for you. There is a green button on the other side to close the pit and stand them upright to untie them. I lied, I love you forever

A Love War: TWISTED

Tyrell, not just 'til death do us part. Take care of our kids...."

"Des, no!" Tyrell pleads even more, but to no avail. Desdemona jumped into the pit of battery acid.

"No!" T.J. yelled.

"Oh my god!" Monica screams as T.J. runs up the steps.

"Why did you push her off the ledge!?!" T.J. shockingly faulted Tyrell for what had just transpired.

"Son I..." Tyrell tried to get his son to see the truth, but T.J. was repeatedly hitting Tyrell wanting to know why he would push his mother off the ledge.

A Love War: TWISTED

Monica, seeing what T.J. was doing ran up the steps to stop him.

"T.J., stop! She jumped! You and I both saw it!"

"Bullshit! He pushed her! He's going to jail!"

Tyrell couldn't believe his ears; his own son was turning on him although they all knew the truth.

"After all I have done for you... You're going to send me to jail on a lie!?!" Tyrell said in astonishment.

"Somebody has to avenge mom's death." T.J. says as he calls the police from his cell phone.

A Love War: TWISTED

"God have mercy on you boy. God have mercy on you." Tyrell replied.

Monica hits the green button, unties Justin and Nicole and calls the ambulance to take them to the hospital. Moments later the police arrive.

"Officers arrest this man! He is the cause of all of this!" T.J. exclaims.

"Officers I can explain everything." Tyrell says trying to get them to see this is all an unfortunate misunderstanding.

Without giving Tyrell the chance to explain, the officer says,

"I'm sorry sir, but we have to take you into custody. We aren't here because he called; a woman by the name of Monica called us saying a man by the name of Tyrell was assaulting her. Is she here? Sir, are you indeed that Tyrell?"

"Officer, I did not assault anyone." Tyrell said defending himself.

"Yes you did and pushed her into the battery acid!" T.J. alleged.

"Officer he is lying!" Monica stated coming to her dad's defense.

"Alright that's enough. Sir, you are under arrest. Anything you say can and will be held against you in the court of law. If you cannot afford an attorney one will be provided for you..."

SIX

YEARS

LATER

A Love War: TWISTED

Chapter 15: The Conversation

Incarcerated in Coastal State Prison, Tyrell has had much time to think. He spends most of his time reminiscing on days of old when everything was well and skeletons were kept in their respective closets.

"God, I messed up. I know I have not been the best of your children, and I know I am probably not high on the priority list, but if you could… just...have a little mercy; just come see about me for a little while, I would sure appreciate it. I wouldn't hold you long. I just need assurance that even a sinner like me can be okay in this world and turn things

around. Forgive me for the things I have done. I need you Lord. Reach through these prison walls and into my heart and take out everything not like you. I want my life back. Please Lord… Hear my humble cry.”

Overheard by his cell mate Tyson, Tyrell continues to cry out to God as he is comforted.

“Brother, God hears you, even in these walls. He's the reason I ain't dead in here, but I have life man. This is where I will die. You know the beauty of it though? This is where I started living. I found God in here at my lowest point. If I can bounce back and face my music, you can too. Don't give up."

Tyrell responds to Tyson through tears and emotion.

"I just don't see how this all happened man. Everything was fine. It seems like just yesterday I was raising my kids and getting ready for them to go off to college. Now for the past 6 years I have been sitting in jail, hopeful that one day some truth would come to this situation and I would be released. Each day gets more and more frustrating. I haven't seen either of my kids, nor have I have I had any contact with their guardians. They're grown now...I wonder how they are doing. I wonder what they are doing."

Tyrell's wonder would soon come to an end with an unexpected visitor.

"Weston! Someone is here to see you! Let's go!" The guard said.

"Someone is here to see me!?! I didn't have any visitors scheduled."

"Looks like new council, or at least she's dressed like a lawyer. Might be something good. Maybe not."

Tyrell goes to the visiting area and waits for his visitor to reveal herself, only to find his heart melting and himself in tears and speechless.

A Love War: TWISTED

"Monica…my baby girl! Father you have answered my prayers! Thank you Lord!"

"Keep it down Weston! There are other people besides you two!"

Monica realizes there is limited time to talk and urges Tyrell to sit down.

"Dad, if you can't tell yes, I have been to law school and I am under a practice. I am working on getting you an appeal and at the least another look at your case. I can't be in on the case because I was a witness, but I can do everything I can to make sure you get a fair shot this time."

Tyrell, excited but doubtful asks,

A Love War: TWISTED

"What about T.J., Nicole and Justin? You know at trial Nicole and Justin knew nothing and T.J., well…. Let's just say he's still my son but I am still healing. Do you really think we have a chance?

"Dad we have more than a chance. I have the letters mom was taunting you with safely tucked away. They have her fingerprints on them I am sure, not to mention they were handwritten. Mom never changed her handwriting or her signature over the years. Plus, this time, she is not here to try to hinder anything. As far as T.J. goes, I have something to tell you… He will be a hard nut to crack. He is a lawyer now too. Auntie Nicole and Uncle Justin told me."

Perplexed and proud, Tyrell asks, "So does that mean he can prosecute?"

"No daddy, he can't because he was a witness too, but it will be hard to get him to not stick to his story. I haven't spoken to him since the day you were convicted. He married Candace I know. I don't know if he has any kids."

"What about you baby girl?" Tyrell asks in anticipation.

"No kids yet. I am still single and mingling."

"So back to business baby, what do I need to do while I am in here?"

A Love War: TWISTED

"It's simple daddy. Right now just continue to be a model prisoner and make sure to continue to stay out of trouble. It will make it very hard to get an appeal if you get in trouble."

The guard signals that Tyrell's time is up. "Weston! Time's up! Let's go!"

"Alright baby girl. Thank you for everything. I am not going to give up okay? I love you. If the Lord is willing I'll see you soon."

"I'll be here every visiting day I can daddy. I love you too. We are going to get you out of here..."

A Love War: TWISTED

Chapter 16: The Confrontation

"Hey baby, how was your day?" Candace said to T.J. as he came into their bedroom, throwing his suitcase in the corner and loosening his tie.

"I don't want to talk about it." T. J. said agitated as usual.

"Another case lost by lack of evidence and weak witnesses. The bitch couldn't even stick to her own story. I don't get it. You were credible up until the day you had to testify and you make me look like an ass in court!"

Candace, trying to be a loving wife and support her husband. did her best to console the distraught T.J..

A Love War: TWISTED

"Baby, you will eventually win some cases. Just stop taking every case you see though. You see what happens when you jump in head first with no knowledge of the case. Do some research before you say yes."

"Yeah, I got jumping in head first like that from my father. That motherfucker. I swear… If I could go back and somehow tell my mom to let me have a different dad…if I had a brain as a sperm organism I promise I would have backstroked…"

Candace, in a loving and soothing voice replies,

"Baby, you can't turn back the hands of time, but you can make yourself a brighter future."

A Love War: TWISTED

"I don't need that positive bullshit right now okay!?! I just...I want to be alone. I'm going downstairs."

Tearing up and discouraged from the lashing out, Candace drops to her knees when he leaves the room and starts to pray.

"Father...Father I don't know what else to do. I have been a good wife these past three years. I have been there for him in ways no one else ever has. He's hit me. He's disgraced me. He's even gotten me to where I don't talk to my own family. I can't even go out with my own mom and sister. He won't even let them come around, even if he is not here. I love him though. I have given up so much.

A Love War: TWISTED

How much more am I supposed to take? Help me Lord.... Help me please."

Meanwhile, the phone rings and Candace is now agitated because she is sure it is the same blocked number that has been calling all day. Finally, she decides to answer once more.

"Hello? Hello? Look, whoever this is I don't know who the hell you are looking for but if you want to play with someone go find a mate, some children, friends or your parents! Quit calling this damn house!"

The other party's response is, "Aaaaahhhhhhhhh!"

A Love War: TWISTED

The scream is so loud in Candace's ear that T.J. hears it. T.J. immediately comes running up the stairs and asks,

"What the hell is going on in here!?! Why the hell are you yelling and shit!?!"

"I didn't yell! Some bitch just screamed in my ear and hung up the phone! The motherfucker has been calling all day and won't stop!"

Again, the phone rings, but this time T.J. answers with anticipation of letting off some steam in the receiver to this individual.

"Look bitch, I don't know who the fuck you think you are screaming in my wife's ear, but apparently you have the wrong number, so I suggest you stop calling here before I have you tracked down! Do you understand me you test tube baby!?! Sorry excuse for a human being! Scream in my ear dammit! Scream in my muthafucking ear and see what the hell happens!"

The individual says "I see you're married now, huh son?"

T.J.'s heart drops to his feet, "Mom...."

Candace overhears T.J. and asks, "What did you say?"

"Nothing bae. I have to take this call okay? I know who it is. It's a witness, she's not all there. Can I have the room bae? Please?"

A Love War: TWISTED

Candace, though suspicious, lets T.J. have the room.

"Fine, but handle this before she gets dealt with. I'm not playing."

"Mom, how the hell did you get my house number!?! I told you to call the cell or my work phone if you need me! What the hell!?!"

"First of all I am your mother. You don't cuss at me. You didn't answer, so I started calling the house. You're just like your father. You love talking in person but can't stand phones."

"That's no excuse. You know I'm a busy man and I have a lot of work at the moment. What do you need?"

A Love War: TWISTED

"I wanted to inform you that your sister saw your dad yesterday. My little friend down at the prison informed me."

Confused and ignorant T.J. replies, "So what does that have to do with anything?"

"She could be trying to get him a pardon and a second look at his case."

"That won't happen. She's not that smart."

"Don't underestimate your sister T.J. She is a lawyer too. Remember you both have my blood."

"But I have the brain. There is no way in hell they will get a second look at his case."

A Love War: TWISTED

"Damnit don't be a fool T.J.! I am telling you this for a reason!"

"Look mama, I appreciate the concern, but we are good, okay? I will handle it if anything comes up. I promise."

"For your sake, I hope you do."

Desdemona hangs up the phone and T.J. is silent for a short time.

T.J. then proceeds downstairs to Candace who is now making dinner.

Eyes puffy and red from crying but trying to think and be positive, Candace asks, "Everything okay baby?"

"Yea bae, everything is fine. So, what's for dinner?"

A Love War: TWISTED

Chapter 17: Wisdom

As Tyrell was reading a book in his cell, slowly drifting off to sleep, he would soon be awakened by another surprise.

"Weston, you have a visitor! C'mon up and at 'em!"

Tyrell, expecting to see Monica once more with some good news, was in for yet another surprise.

"I hope she's here to tell me that things are moving Lord. Please, I need this…"

As Tyrell walks into the visiting area, he scans the area looking for his daughter, only to find,

A Love War: TWISTED

"Mom!?! What are you doing here!?!".

"I told you one day I would come to see you. Sit down, we don't have much time."

"Mama…I told you I never wanted you to see me like this…"

"And I told you I never wanted to see you in this type of situation because of what you were doing, so it looks like we both didn't care about what the other one said. Look at cha, all ruddy and beard all long and whatnot. Boy, you do realize that life don't stop just because you locked up? You played a dangerous hand with them drugs trying to cover it up with an pharmaceutical job, and in the end what did you end up with?"

Tyrell, almost at the point of tears from facing his mother could only reply, "Nothing mama."

"Wrong again baby. You ended up with everything you needed. You have God and he's giving you time. Just because you in here and they say you doing hard time doesn't mean it has to be a true statement. Your time is what you make of it baby, so how are you spending it?"

"Well mama, I'm reading and working out a lot. I am keeping my nose clean and Monica is trying to get me out of here. Mama, I didn't kill her. I put that on everything I love."

"Baby, I know you didn't. One thing a mama will always know is her children. You get squeamish at the site of dead meat and pass out at the site of blood. Ain't no way you could have pushed that woman from there and not have nearly fell over in there yourself or passed out."

"Well mama, you know the story goes I allegedly pushed her into that battery acid. You know T.J. turned on me and that is the real reason I am in here. I'm still heartbroken by it. I don't know what to do mama. I want my life back, the right way this time. Mama, what do I do in a situation like this? I have been trying to keep faith in God, but I just don't think he hears me in this situation. I know Monica is trying to help me and I know I have been a model citizen in here and I am innocent, so why am I still in here!?! What the hell did I do to deserve this!?! I'm not perfect, but who is!?!

"Boy you sit yourself down and pull yourself together right now! I ain't raise no weak-minded son and I ain't finna stand for this from you! Now you wipe them tears so God can show you the way. You hear me!?! Your daddy didn't die for you to live this way. He didn't die in war for you to quit! If he were here right now, boy you would be as distinguished as a Colonel in the army for 30 years! I'm sorry I couldn't be what he could to you, but I did the best I could! Now if you don't owe anyone else something you owe God a thank you that you didn't get killed and you owe me 42 years of life! You come from a long line of people who never took no for an answer and I expect nothing less of you. You have king's blood running warm in your veins. I don't care how cold the world gets! Now get determination in your mind and a lion in your heart and break through those chains that have you bound! You hear what I say!?!

Tyrell, humbled by his mom's words says, "Yes, ma'am".

A Love War: TWISTED

"Now.. I ain't no lawyer and I ain't got no fancy degrees and such, but one thing I do have that is lacking in today's world is a strong faith and a determine spirit. Baby, I ain't never seen the righteous forsaken. Do you know you probably around plenty of innocent men in here? Hoodwinked and swindled by the system just like you in sticky situations and they done gave up hope. God can get you out of here, but it all starts with you baby. There is nothing impossible with him, but without him…you are just like the rest of them in here. So what you gone do? Are you gone sit on the stool of do-nothin' or are you gone stand up, pull your pants up and stand steadfast on what you know to be true?"

Tyrell almost at the point of tears in inspiration replies,

"Mama, you always know what to say…I'm sorry all of this had to happen. I am going to be the man God called me to be, for real this time. I will get out of here and I will get my life back."

"Weston, time's up! Let's go!"

Gloria, sad to see her son Tyrell go back behind prison walls, leaves him a few more words of wisdom before departing.

"Remember baby, God has a plan for your life. Remember Jeremiah 29:11. Until your plan matches up with his nothing you do will prosper. I love you and I will see you soon."

"Love you too mama. Thanks for coming. I needed that..."

A Love War: TWISTED

Chapter 18: Forming the Plans

After a long day at the firm, Monica decides to take a drive to Justin and Nicole's to clear her mind and start fresh in the morning.

Upon her arrival, she knocks on the door and becomes suspicious when there is no answer.

"I wonder where they could be?" says Monica as she uses her spare key to get in.

"Unc? Auntie? Where y'all at?"

Monica proceeds through the house looking for Justin and Nicole to find a shocking discovery.

A Love War: TWISTED

Upon entering the master bedroom, Monica finds Justin and Nicole beaten, bloodied, barely breathing and tied up. Justin is conscious, but Nicole is knocked out.

"Oh my gosh! Who did this to you!?! I'm calling the ambulance right now!

After untying them, Justin begins to speak with long breaths in between from being bound and gagged.

"Monica....you're not going to.....believe this but.... Your mother....

Before Justin could finish, Monica tells him,

A Love War: TWISTED

"Don't say another word unc. I've got this. Everything is going to be okay. She wants a fight…she's got one!"

Meanwhile on the other side of town, T.J. and Candace are out having a romantic dinner when T.J. gets yet another call.

"Baby you look beautiful tonight; you look good enough to die for."

With a twinkle in her eyes, Candace replies, "Aww thank you baby. You don't look to bad yourself. You know I love you in brown."

In the midst of the romantic conversation, T.J.'s phone rings.

"Hold on baby, let me take this call."

A Love War: TWISTED

"Now baby? We're having such a good time."

"What did I say!?!"

Candace is once again intimidated and heartbroken by T.J.'s temper and words. She starts to cry but immediately wipes her tears and scurries to the bathroom.

"Mom, what do you need? Make it quick. I'm with my wife."

"You're lucky I haven't come after her. You know I hate that bitch."

"Mom, I swear if you lay a hand on her…"

"Calm down boy. I'm calling because you don't have to worry about

A Love War: TWISTED

Nicole and Justin when we go to trial. They are taken care of."

T.J. pauses and hears his heartbeat for a couple of seconds awestruck by his mother's statement.

"What did you say…?"

"They are…"

"I heard you! How could you do that!?! They raised me when even you or dad couldn't be there! They had nothing to do with this! What the fuck!?! What the fuck!?!"

"Do you want to spend the rest of your life in prison for perjury!?! I don't think so! Last time I checked, I was dead to the world, literally! Desdemona is dead.

A Love War: TWISTED

You know I am now Anastasia. I'm trying to help you when this goes to trial again"

"What are you talking about!?! What are you telling me!?!"

"Stupid I'm telling you that there is nothing I can do about this not going to trial. There is evidence against me and there is reason to believe that you lied to the police and on the stand!"

"I ain't worried. I have never lost a case and I don't plan on losing one now!"

"That's not what your record says boy. You'd better start doing your research now."

A Love War: TWISTED

T.J. hangs up the phone in fury only to turn around with the whole restaurant looking at him and his wife Candace in awe.

"Baby…is everything okay?"

"Um…yeah. Let's go home bae… let's go home."

A Love War: TWISTED

Chapter 19: The Deal

While at Shining Waters Hospital,
Monica is at a breaking point; heartbroken
by the condition of her once guardians. She
holds the necklace while she cries, trembles
and prays.

**"God please let them be okay.
They are all I have right now. I can't take
much more of..."**

Monica's prayer is interrupted by a
phone call from a private number. As she
answers she is thrown into a frenzy by the
caller.

"Hey baby. I know you are mad at
me for what I did to them but let me
explain..."

A Love War: TWISTED

Monica replies with anger,

"Look I don't know how you got my number and I don't really care, but now you are going down! Do you hear me?!?! You are going to be under the jail!"

"There is no need for all of that sweetheart. I only called to give you an easy way out of all of this. There is no need for this to go to trial and all of these legal fees and such to come into play. This is my proposal. You give me the evidence and I will make sure your dad will be released."

Monica, thinking of the proposal and all of the pros and cons replies.

A Love War: TWISTED

"How do I know you aren't just going to have him killed as soon as he gets out?"

"If I wanted him killed, I would have done it while he was in there baby. I just want my name cleared. You give me the evidence, it disappears, along with me. Then he gets out the next day. No questions asked. Just meet me on 912 Oaks Drive at midnight on Thursday with the evidence. Yes, I just gave you my place of residence because I trust you. So trust me daughter of mine for once in your life."

"Yeah, in your dreams, but I will be there."

A Love War: TWISTED

Monica then enters the room again to Nicole and Justin. They are conscious and able to talk.

"I'm going to see dad. Are y'all going to be alright?"

Justin replies, "Yeah baby girl we will be okay. Just some scratches and bruises."

Nicole replies, "Baby, I gave you that necklace for a reason. It belonged to your mother at first. Do what you have to do and remember we love you."

"I love y'all too. Call me if y'all get discharged."

Monica then hurries to the prison before visiting hours are over to consult with her dad on this proposal and the decision she is going to make. Upon her arrival, she sees that her grandmother is also there visiting Tyrell.

"Well mama, I have actually been doing pretty good. They were talking about putting me in a different cell block with more positive people to help me with my surroundings and give me more free time. Monica, baby! It must be my lucky day!

"Dad I have something to tell you…"

Tyrell, with his heart beating in anticipation and desire of good news says, "What is it baby girl?"

"Mom gave me a deal to grant your freedom."

A Love War: TWISTED

"Baby you know that's a trap. You know she can't be trusted." Gloria says.

"Grandma I know but what am I supposed to do? If she doesn't get this evidence, she is going to have daddy killed in here."

Tyrell responds, "Baby girl, I have lived life. I know what love is all about and sometimes you just have to face the music like Tyson told me. If death is the end for me, then so-be-it."

"Now don't you talk that way about this boy. I told you remember Jeremiah 29:11. We got this covered. Now come on Monica. Time is up here. We have much to discuss on what you gone do to get yo'

daddy outta here..."

Chapter 20: Denied Transaction

Around 11:55 p.m., Monica parks across the street from the destination of where Anastasia, told her to meet her. At 11:57, she receives a text from her saying,

"I see your car. Come on when you are ready."

Pulsating, knowing what's at stake, Monica gets out of the car and walks slowly across the street.

Upon knocking just once, the door opens to a long hallway and a shadowy figure at the end of it.

"Come and sit my child. We have much to discuss. The shadowy figure says while moving to the next room.

A Love War: TWISTED

Monica takes a deep breath and follows the figure to what seems to be the living room.

As she enters, she finally sees her mother's face.

"Why do you have gloves on?" says Anastasia.

Monica replies, "I always wear gloves. Keeps dust and germs off of my hands."

Anastasia replies, "Smart, very smart. So I take it that's the evidence in that folder?"

"Yes, but before you retrieve this from me, I would like security on how you are going to get dad out of jail."

A Love War: TWISTED

Anastasia pulls out a cell phone, "All I have to do is make one phone call."

"Make the call."

"Not 'til I see the evidence"

Monica gives the folder to Anastasia.

"Okay and this is indeed the original copy?"

"Yes, now make the call. You have your evidence."

"Okay. Ted, let him out. Yeah, I have the paperwork and she about to get dealt with."

"So you were never a woman of your word. Dad was right. Ted...I know him. I figured he was crooked."

A Love War: TWISTED

"Shut up because if you figured all of this, you would not be in this predicament."

"What predicament?"

Anastasia pulls out a gun on Monica.

"So you'd shoot me rather than fight me like a real woman? They say anything worth having is worth fighting for."

Anastasia, offended by Monica's comment, puts down the gun and charges for Monica. Anastasia misses her tackle and hits the end table and is punched twice by Monica and then dragged up the stairs to the master bedroom.

A Love War: TWISTED

"I wish you would have jumped in battery acid for real! This would not be happening!"

As Monica goes for a clubbing blow, Anastasia hits her in the stomach. Stunned for a while Monica is trying to fight off Anastasia while she is choking her.

"I hate I ever had a daughter, especially one as ugly and stupid as you!" Anastasia says delivering a punch to Monica on the jaw.

Anastasia then walks slowly to the drawer to retrieve her sword. She unsheathes it and walks slowly towards Monica only to get yet another surprise from behind.

A Love War: TWISTED

"Bitch!" Nicole says as she hit Anastasia in the back of the head.

"Motherfucker! Imma beat yo ass!"

Justin then pulls Nicole off of Anastasia while Monica rises to reveal yet another surprise.

T.J. stabs Justin with the sword Anastasia dropped.

"I always hated you," T.J. says as Justin drops to the floor. "Between you and my dad I don't know who I hated more."

Monica then punches Anastasia twice in the face, once in the stomach and says, "This is for daddy. Now you charge this to my head and not my heart." Monica then rips the necklace from her neck and

A Love War: TWISTED

kicks Anastasia in the stomach out of the window onto the concrete sidewalk below.

After looking at Anastasia's motionless body on the sidewalk bleeding slowly from the fall, she spits from the broken window hoping it will hit her.

"After all of these years, you didn't think I knew that necklace was a tracking device. I love you still, even though you were one crazy bitch. I wish this could have ended differently."

T.J. tries to run but is stopped by Candace who has picked up the gun Anastasia had downstairs.

"I can't take anymore T.J. You have hurt me for the last time. I'm sorry."

A Love War: TWISTED

Candace shoots T.J. four times in the chest.

Crying uncontrollably, Candace begs God, **"Father, please forgive me."**

Monica comforts Candace, "He will sweetheart…he will.

Meanwhile, Nicole is holding Justin as he dies in her arms.

"Don't cry baby. I now know what life and love is all about. I am so happy to have lived the rest of my life with you and I am so happy it ended with the last face I see being yours. I love baby. This isn't goodbye this is see you later. I love…"

"He didn't die in vain." Monica said. "Let's get out of here."

Chapter 21: Sunshine

Anastasia's call was not a bluff. Tyrell was released the next day with all charges dropped and no felonies on his record. After 6 years of waiting and being patient, Tyrell was finally free.

"How do you feel dad?" Monica asked.

"New…as if life has just begun for me. I am still coping with getting up on my own and going to bed on my own but I am sure it will come with time, much like eating on my own too. Just pray for me sweetheart."

"Baby, this is a blessing beyond measure. You can start over with a new life now. And we are all here to support you." Gloria says.

Tyrell took a second to look out at the bay, reminiscing on all of his endeavors over the past 16 years.

"God I know that I have not been the best of your children, but I am ready to do what I need to do for you. I have my mom, my daughter and you on my side. I am ready and willing to do this thing the right way."

Nicole says, "You can do it. I am here for you too."

"Nicole, I'm…"

"No, it's okay. It is for the best. He is resting in peace. Let's just move on."

A Love War: TWISTED

Tyrell hugs Nicole as she, Gloria, Monica and Tyrell walk the beach laughing...

ABOUT THE AUTHOR

Rowdy D. Solomon Jr. "(Sol) was born in Macon, Ga. on November 20th 1991. He is proud military veteran pursuing a career in writing and journalism.

He has been writing for a total of six years and has finally published his first book.

We hope you enjoy.

Author R. D. Solomon Jr.